My Secret Unicorn

Flying High

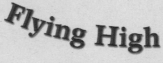

D0168615

My Secret Unicorn
Flying High

Linda Chapman

Illustrated by Biz Hull

Cover Illustration by Andrew Farley

A LITTLE
APPLE
PAPERBACK

SCHOLASTIC INC.
New York   Toronto   London   Auckland   Sydney
Mexico City   New Delhi   Hong Kong   Buenos Aires

ISBN 0-439-81384-0

12 11 10 9 8 7 6 5 4 3 2 1   6 7 8 9 10 11/0

Printed in the U.S.A.   40

To Suzy Higgins—
you would be
a wonderful unicorn friend

Flying High

CHAPTER

One

Lauren Foster sat at the desk in her bedroom and sighed. The sun was just disappearing behind the Blue Ridge Mountains and the pale blue sky was streaked with pink and gold. In the paddock behind the house, her pony, Twilight, lifted his head and looked up. How she wished she could be with him, but she had work to do. Mr. Noland, her teacher, had told the class that they were going to do a project on the local mountain range. It had sounded like fun, particularly when he had said that they could work with their friends. However, now that she was faced with drawing a map of all the mountains, streams, and valleys, Lauren was quickly getting bored with the whole project.

She pushed her long, blond hair back behind her ears and wondered how her friends Mel and Jessica were doing. Jessica was supposed to be drawing pictures of all the animals that lived in the mountains, and Mel was going to draw the trees and plants that grew there. Lauren chewed her pencil and looked at the blank piece

of paper in front of her. She had definitely gotten the hardest part!

It wasn't even as if she could ask her mom and dad for help. Her mom was busy working in the den, and her dad was out at a meeting on farming. She'd checked the bookshelves but there didn't seem to be any books that might help.

And she couldn't use the computer because her mom was working on it.

Lauren made up her mind. It was way too nice an evening to be inside. She could finish the map later. Jumping to her feet, she grabbed her jacket and hurried out of the room.

As she passed the bedroom of her younger brother, Max, she could hear a story-tape playing. She walked down the hall and peered around the den door. "I'm just going out to see Twilight, Mom," she said.

Alice Foster was typing quickly, her eyes fixed on the computer screen. She was a children's book author and at the moment she was in the middle of writing a new story. "OK, honey," she answered vaguely, not even looking around. "Don't stay out too late."

"I won't," Lauren replied. With a feeling of relief, she ran down the stairs and out the back door.

When Twilight saw Lauren coming down the path, he whinnied and trotted over to meet her.

Lauren's face broke into a smile, as it always did at the sight of him. "Hi, boy," she said.

Twilight stamped one hoof. With his shaggy mane and scruffy dappled coat, he looked just like any other small gray pony. But he wasn't. Lauren's fingers closed around the hair from his mane that she always kept in her pocket and a familiar sense of excitement tingled through her veins. She glanced around. There was no one nearby. It was safe.

Clutching the hair, Lauren began to whisper the words she knew so well.

Twilight Star, Twilight Star,
Twinkling high above so far.
Shining light, shining bright,
Will you grant my wish tonight?
Let my little horse forlorn
Be at last a unicorn!

As Lauren spoke the final word, there was a bright purple flash that made her shut her eyes. When she opened them again, Twilight was standing in front of her. But he wasn't a gray pony anymore — he was a snowy-white unicorn.

"It worked!" Lauren exclaimed in delight. She'd said the spell many times in the past few weeks since she'd discovered Twilight's hidden powers. Even so, she still couldn't help thinking that one day nothing was going to happen.

"What did you expect?" Twilight said with a toss of his head. His pearly white horn caught the last rays of the setting sun, and his silver mane and tail shone. He blew on her hands. "I thought you weren't coming to see me this evening. You said you had homework to do." His lips didn't move, but Lauren could hear him clearly in her head.

"I still have homework to do," Lauren said. "I've got to draw this map of the mountains. But it's really hard." She sighed. "I don't know what I'm going to do. I told Mel and Jessica that I'd have it done by tomorrow."

"But that's easy," Twilight exclaimed. "I can fly you over the mountains, and you can draw them as we go."

Lauren stared at him. "Really?"

"Of course," Twilight said, tossing his mane.

Lauren grinned. "Oh, Twilight, you're the best. Come on. Let's go!"

★　★　★

Five minutes later, Lauren and Twilight were cantering through the sky. The wind whipped Lauren's long hair back from her face, but she didn't feel cold. Twilight's silver mane swirled around her, and his body was warm. As they swooped over the mountains, she laughed out loud. Flying with Twilight was the greatest feeling ever!

Lauren took a pen and paper out of her pocket and began to draw everything she could see. The wind pulled at the paper, and she had to hang on tight to stop it from blowing away. She was grateful for Twilight's special unicorn magic that kept her from falling off.

"OK, I've drawn the river and the

valleys," she said, straining her eyes through the gathering darkness. "Can we go a little lower so that I can see the trees?"

"I can do better than that," Twilight said. "Why don't I fly low enough for you to collect some leaves from them?"

"Wow!" Lauren said with delight. "I could stick them onto the poster next to Mel's drawings."

Twilight cantered down through the sky and landed on the soft forest floor. Lauren picked a leaf from every different type of tree and bush she could find — pine, poplar, wild cherry, dogwood — as well as others for which she didn't know the names.

"This is great!" she said, getting on

Twilight's back. "Our project's going to be the best."

As Twilight trotted forward, Lauren caught sight of two white-tailed deer standing in the shadows of the trees. They were staring at Twilight in astonishment. Lauren grinned at the surprise on their faces.

"Where to now?" Twilight asked as he kicked with his back legs and plunged upward. It was getting very dark.

"We'd better go home," Lauren said reluctantly. That was the problem with taking Twilight for a ride when he was a unicorn — it was only safe at night when they wouldn't be seen by anyone, and that meant that their rides couldn't go on for too long. Mrs. Fontana, the lady who had first told Lauren that unicorns existed, had warned her that she must never let Twilight's secret be discovered by anyone because it would put him in danger.

"Here we go," Twilight said, jumping over a treetop as he cantered upward. "Hang on!"

Back at Granger's Farm, Twilight landed safely in his paddock.

"Thank you!" Lauren told him, giving him a hug.

"You're welcome," Twilight said, nuzzling her. "It was fun."

Lauren said the words of the Undoing

Spell. There was a purple flash and, suddenly, Twilight was a pony again.

"Good night, boy," Lauren whispered, patting him on the neck. And then she ran into the house.

To her relief, her dad wasn't back and her mom was still working. Lauren crept up the stairs and hurriedly changed into her pajamas. She glanced at her bedroom clock. It was nine o'clock, but she didn't feel tired. That was one of the things she'd found out about flying with Twilight — she never felt tired when she got back. *Maybe it's one of his magical powers,* she thought, as she pulled the roughly drawn map out of her pocket and began to copy it onto a larger piece of paper.

As she worked, she thought about Twilight's magical powers. Mrs. Fontana had told her that it was up to every unicorn to discover those powers for itself. Lauren and Twilight had already found out that he was able to make others feel brave when he touched them with his horn. But it was exciting to think that he might have other powers that they still hadn't discovered.

I wonder what they are, Lauren thought, as she finished drawing the last few mountains on the map. Then she heard her mom's study door open. She threw down her pencil, turned off her light, and jumped into bed.

CHAPTER

Two

"This is totally awesome!" Mel exclaimed as she looked at Lauren's map the next morning.

Lauren grinned happily. She'd gotten up early to finish the map and, although it wasn't completely colored in yet, she had to admit that it looked good. As well as the streams and valleys, she'd drawn a few interesting trees and plants she'd seen.

"I've got these, too," she said, taking the leaves out of her schoolbag. "I thought we could paste them around the edges."

"Wow!" Mel said, her brown eyes widening. "Where did you get those?"

"Oh . . . just around," Lauren said vaguely. She changed the subject quickly. "What do you think, Jessica?" she asked, looking at their other friend.

Jessica's head was lowered. She was biting her fingernails and didn't seem to hear Lauren's question.

Mel waved the map under her nose. "Hey, Jessica. What do you think of Lauren's map?"

"Yeah, yeah — it's great," Jessica said, not really looking at it.

Lauren frowned. "Are you OK?" she asked.

"I'm fine!" Jessica snapped.

Lauren and Mel exchanged surprised glances. It wasn't like Jessica to be mean.

Lauren sat down beside her. "Want to tell us about it?" she asked with concern.

Jessica's shoulders sagged. "I'm sorry. It's just . . . well, things aren't very good at home right now."

"What's wrong?" Mel asked, sitting down on the other side of her.

"Sally's coming to stay for the weekend," Jessica replied.

"But I thought you liked Sally," Lauren said.

Jessica's mom had died when she was

little, and Sally was her dad's fiancée. They were getting married in two weeks.

Jessica sighed. "I do like her. But she's also bringing Samantha, her daughter. Samantha usually stays with her dad when Sally comes to stay, but she'll be living with us after the wedding. So Sally thought she should come and stay this weekend." Jessica swallowed. "I'm dreading it. I know Samantha doesn't like me."

Lauren took Jessica's hand and squeezed it. "I'm sure she does, Jessica. It won't be that bad."

Jessica looked down at the desk again. She didn't seem convinced.

Nothing seemed to cheer Jessica up that afternoon, not even Mr. Noland telling them that their poster was great.

At the end of the day, Lauren, Mel, and Jessica walked to the school gate together.

"Mom, Dad, and I are flying to Florida tonight," Mel said. "We always go to see my aunt and uncle every Memorial Day weekend."

"What about Shadow?" Lauren asked, thinking about Mel's pony. "Who's taking care of him?"

"Brad," said Mel. Brad was one of the men who worked on her parents' farm. "I'll miss Shadow lots, but it'll be fun being away. Mom said we might even go to Disney World! I'll see you when I get back," Mel finished, waving as she walked over to join her parents at the school gate.

"Wow!" Lauren said. She turned to see Jessica's reaction, but Jessica hadn't heard. She was staring straight ahead. Lauren followed her gaze. Jessica's dad was standing with Sally by the gate, and with them was a slim girl who looked about eleven years old. She had sleek, dark-brown hair and a sulky expression on her face.

For a moment, Lauren almost thought that Jessica was going to turn around and run back into the classroom. But just then Mr. Parker stepped forward.

"Jessica!" he called. "Over here!"

Jessica had no choice but to go over. Lauren followed her.

"Hi, girls," Sally said to them. "Did you have a good day?"

"Yes, thanks," Lauren said.

Jessica just nodded.

Lauren looked at Samantha. The older girl was scuffing one of her sneakers across the ground. Her brown hair hid

her face, and it was impossible to guess what she was thinking. She didn't look at Jessica once.

"Well," Mr. Parker said, after a pause, "I guess we should be getting home."

"Dad," Jessica said suddenly, "can Lauren come over this weekend?"

Lauren looked at her in surprise.

"I don't know, Jess," Mr. Parker began, looking a bit awkward. "Another time might be better. We have Samantha staying. . . ."

Samantha kicked a stone. "I don't care if she has a friend come over."

"Samantha!" Sally said, and for a moment Lauren thought she was going to be mad at Samantha. But then Sally's face softened. "Please don't use that tone of voice," she said mildly.

Samantha shrugged and kicked the ground again.

"Please, Dad," Jessica begged.

Her dad looked at Samantha, then sighed. "OK." He turned to Lauren. "You're very welcome to come over tomorrow morning, Lauren — if it's all right with your mom and dad. Now, we'd better go. Come on, Jessica — the car's parked around the corner."

As Lauren watched Jessica and her family walk out of sight, she felt a little sad. She wouldn't want to be Jessica this weekend.

★   ★   ★

As soon as Lauren got home from school, she changed clothes and went outside to meet Twilight. As she groomed him, she told him about Jessica. He couldn't speak to her when he wasn't a unicorn, but she knew he understood.

"Jessica's so unhappy," Lauren told him, as she swept the brush over his neck.

Twilight nickered sympathetically.

"I'm going over there tomorrow morning. I just wish there was something I could do to cheer her up," Lauren said.

Twilight pushed her with his nose. Lauren frowned. She had a feeling he was trying to tell her something. Twilight nudged at his saddle hanging on the fence. Lauren's eyes widened. Of course!

"I can bring Jessica back here tomorrow, and she can ride you!" she exclaimed. "She loves horses. It's bound to cheer her up."

Twilight nodded as if that was exactly what he'd been trying to say.

CHAPTER

Three

"Hi, Lauren," Mr. Parker said when Lauren arrived at Jessica's house the next morning. "Jessica's in the kitchen with Sally and Samantha."

Lauren walked into the large kitchen. Jessica was sitting at the table, drawing a picture of a horse. Samantha was listening to a Discman. Her eyes were closed.

"Lauren!" Jessica said, jumping up.

Sally was unloading the dishwasher. "Hi, Lauren. How are you?"

"Fine, thanks," Lauren replied. She looked at Jessica's drawing. "I like your horse."

"Thanks," Jessica said, smiling.

"My little artist," Mr. Parker said fondly as he came to look at her picture.

Jessica shot an embarrassed look at Lauren. "Come on, let's go to my room."

"Do you want to take some milk and cookies with you?" Sally asked.

Lauren and Jessica both nodded eagerly and, while Sally poured two glasses of milk for them, Jessica got the cookie jar.

"Do you want one, Samantha?" Jessica offered.

But Samantha continued to listen to her Discman, her eyes still closed.

Sally removed the headphones from Samantha's ears.

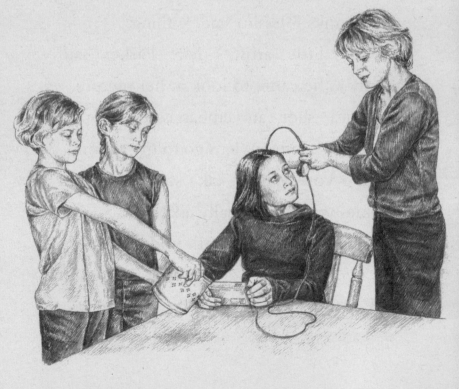

"Mom!" Samantha protested.

"Jessica just asked you if you would like a cookie," Sally said.

Samantha looked in the jar that Jessica was holding out. "I don't like any of them," she said rudely.

Lauren stared. If she'd spoken like that, her mom would have been furious with her, but Sally didn't say anything.

"What kind of cookies do you like, Samantha?" Mr. Parker asked.

Samantha shrugged. "Pecan and chocolate chip."

"Well, in that case we should get some when we're out this afternoon," he said.

"Come on," Jessica muttered to Lauren. "Let's go to my room."

When they reached Jessica's bedroom, Jessica flung herself down on her bed. "I can't believe how Dad and Sally treat Samantha. She gets her own way with everything. Like this afternoon, Dad suggested we all go for a game of miniature golf or bowling, but no, Samantha doesn't want to do that so we have to spend the afternoon shopping at the mall instead." Jessica pulled her knees up to her chest. "We always do what she wants to do. What's it going to be like after Dad's wedding when she lives here all the time?"

Lauren wanted to comfort her, but she couldn't think of anything to say.

Jessica sniffed and angrily brushed a tear from her eye. "I'm sorry," she said.

"It's OK," Lauren replied. She remembered her plan from the day before. "Look, why don't we go over to my house and ride Twilight?"

Jessica's eyes lit up. "Yeah — OK!"

They quickly drank their milk, ate their cookies, and took their empty glasses downstairs.

Sally and Samantha were still in the kitchen. Sally was holding Samantha's hands. She broke off as Lauren and Jessica walked in. "Oh . . . hi, girls."

Samantha didn't say anything.

Jessica ignored her. "May Lauren and I go and see Twilight?" she asked Sally.

Sally smiled. "Sure," she said. Then she glanced at Samantha. "Samantha, why don't you go with them? You'd like to see Lauren's pony, wouldn't you?"

Lauren stared at Sally in surprise. This hadn't been part of the plan at all. Anyway, she was sure Samantha would refuse.

Samantha shrugged. "I guess I *could* go," she said.

"I'm sure you'll all have a great time together," Sally said, beaming happily.

Samantha stood up and looked at Lauren and Jessica. "Let's go," she said abruptly. And with that, she walked out of the kitchen.

Shooting looks of dismay at each other, Lauren and Jessica followed Samantha outside.

"Where's your house?" Samantha said to Lauren.

"About ten minutes away," Lauren replied. "It's called Granger's Farm."

"Right." Samantha put her headphones on and walked off down the road ahead of them.

"I don't want her to come!" Jessica said to Lauren.

Lauren shook her head, looking at Samantha striding ahead, and whispered, "But what can we do?"

CHAPTER

Four

Samantha was waiting for them outside the entrance to Granger's Farm.

"Twilight's down there," Lauren said, pointing to the path that led around the side of the farmhouse to the paddock.

Samantha shrugged as if she wasn't interested, but followed Lauren and Jessica down the path.

Twilight was standing by the paddock gate. He whinnied as he saw them.

"Oh, he's beautiful!" The words burst out of Samantha.

Both Lauren and Jessica turned to stare. Samantha's face had lit up.

"Do you like horses?" Jessica asked her.

But the delight was already leaving Samantha's face. She shrugged. "They're OK," she said coldly. Then she walked over to the fence and began to kick at a stone.

Lauren decided to ignore her. She got Twilight's halter and grooming kit. She and Jessica groomed Twilight together while Samantha leaned against the fence.

But when Lauren and Jessica went up

to the tack room to fetch Twilight's
saddle and bridle, Lauren saw Samantha
go over to Twilight and stroke his neck.

After they tacked up Twilight, Lauren
let Jessica ride first. Twilight behaved
perfectly for Jessica. He cantered around

the paddock and then jumped over a small fence that Lauren's dad had made.

"Wow!" Jessica said, as she trotted him back to the gate. "Twilight's great, Lauren. He felt like he was flying when he jumped!"

Twilight gave Lauren a playful look from under his long forelock.

Jessica dismounted. "Are you going to ride now, Lauren?"

Lauren nodded, but as she reached to take Twilight's reins, he stepped forward and snorted in Samantha's direction.

Lauren guessed what he was trying to say. "Samantha, would you like to ride Twilight?" she said.

"Me?" Samantha looked very surprised.

For a moment, Lauren thought she was going to say yes, but then she seemed to think better of it. "No, no, I won't," she said abruptly and, crossing her arms, she turned away.

Lauren frowned. She had a feeling Samantha liked horses. But why was she being so unfriendly? She shrugged and glanced at Twilight. He seemed to have a puzzled look on his face, too.

Samantha hardly said another word for the rest of the morning. She ignored Lauren and Jessica as they untacked Twilight and brushed him down. "We should go, Jessica," Samantha said at last. "It's almost lunchtime."

Jessica nodded reluctantly.

As Samantha strode back up the path, Jessica turned to Lauren. "I wish you were coming with us," she said. "The rest of the weekend's going to be awful."

"It might not be that bad," Lauren said, trying to cheer her friend up. "Maybe Samantha will stop being so moody."

Jessica didn't look convinced.

"Come on, Jessica," Samantha called irritably from halfway up the driveway.

"Bye, Lauren," Jessica whispered, suddenly sounding as if she was fighting back tears. She gave Twilight a last pat. "I'd better go."

Lauren watched her run up the path after Samantha. "Oh, Twilight," she said quietly, petting him. "I wish we could help."

That evening, Lauren said the magic words and Twilight turned into a unicorn again. "If only there was something we could do to make Samantha and Jessica get along better," she said. "Samantha's so mean."

"You know, Samantha was petting me when you and Jessica weren't there," Twilight said. "She was different then. I got the feeling that she was a little sad."

"But why should she be sad?" Lauren said. "I mean, I know her mom's getting married again, but Jessica and her dad are really nice." She frowned. "And even if she is sad, she shouldn't be so mean to Jessica."

"I know," Twilight said. "But it must be hard for Samantha to move into a new house and adjust to life with a new father and stepsister."

"I guess," Lauren reluctantly agreed.

"I think Samantha's just putting on an act," Twilight continued. "I don't think she's really mean. People do strange things when they're unhappy."

"Well, I wish Samantha would stop it," Lauren said. "Jessica's really upset."

Twilight nuzzled her. "Look, why don't we go flying?"

Lauren sighed. "OK," she agreed. Maybe that would take her mind off

Jessica's problems for a while. "Let's go to the clearing."

"OK," Twilight agreed eagerly.

Lauren climbed onto his back and he cantered upward into the night sky.

A few minutes later, Twilight flew down between the trees that covered the mountain behind Granger's Farm. He landed lightly on springy grass.

"Wow!" Lauren gasped.

She had never been to the clearing at night before. She had expected it to be dark, but it was lit by hundreds of fireflies. They circled and swooped like tiny moving stars. Lauren slid off Twilight's warm back and breathed in the night air.

It was sweet with the heavy scent of the purple flowers that dotted the grass. They were star-shaped, and at the tip of each petal, a golden spot glowed.

Moonflowers, Lauren thought to herself. She had needed a moonflower when she had first said the spell to turn Twilight into a unicorn. Leaving Twilight, she crouched down and looked at them.

With a soft snort, Twilight moved to the grassy mound at the center of the clearing. Lowering his head, he began to graze, his long horn touching the grass.

Lauren walked over to him and, for the first time, she noticed that there were some rocks around the base of the mound. In the light from the fireflies they seemed to twinkle and shine with a pink glow. "Are these magic rocks?" she asked Twilight.

"I don't think so," Twilight replied. "They're just made of rose quartz. You can find them all through this forest."

"Oh." Lauren couldn't help feeling a little disappointed. She sat down on the grassy mound and watched the fireflies dancing. "I wonder what Jessica's doing now," she said. "I wish I knew."

"Me, too," Twilight said. As he spoke, his horn touched one of the pink rocks. There was a bright purple flash. Twilight shot backward with a startled whinny as mist suddenly started to swirl over the rock.

Lauren leaped to her feet. "Twilight!" she gasped.

CHAPTER

Five

Lauren and Twilight stared at the mist in astonishment.

"What's happening?" Lauren asked, clutching Twilight's mane.

"I don't know," Twilight replied quickly. The mist started fading into the air.

"Look!" Lauren exclaimed. The surface of the rock was shining like a mirror. It had a picture in it. Lauren edged closer. "There are four people," she gasped. "A man, a woman, and . . ." She broke off and stared. "Twilight! It's Jessica's house!"

Twilight moved quickly beside her and together they gazed in astonishment at the image on the rock's surface. It was a picture of the main room at Jessica's house. Mr. Parker and Sally were sitting on the sofa talking to Samantha. Jessica was sitting by herself on the floor.

Lauren could hear a low, buzzing noise. It sounded like voices coming from far, far away. She leaned nearer to the rock. It *was* voices! Now that she was closer to the picture, she could hear what everyone was saying. . . .

Sally was speaking to Samantha. "What
would you like to do tomorrow, darling?"

Lauren saw Samantha shrug. "Go to
the mall," she replied.

"Oh, not again!" Jessica said.

Lauren saw Sally and Mr. Parker exchange anxious looks. "Maybe we could do something else, Sam," said Mr. Parker.

Samantha's face looked rebellious. "There's nothing else worth doing in this stupid town!" she exclaimed.

Lauren looked around at Twilight. "This is amazing!" she whispered. "We're watching what's going on in Jessica's house right now. This rock must be magic after all."

"Maybe it's not the rock," Twilight said thoughtfully. "You said you wished you knew what was going on at Jessica's house, and I touched the rock with my horn. . . ."

"So maybe it's your horn that's making the magic," Lauren guessed.

Twilight nodded. "When I was a foal, my mother used to tell me about the wise Golden Unicorns who rule Arcadia," he said.

"That's the land where all the magic creatures live, isn't it?" Lauren asked, remembering that she had read about Arcadia in the unicorn book she owned.

"Yes," Twilight replied. "My mother told me that there are seven Golden Unicorns. They watch over the human world using a stone table that shines like a mirror when they touch it with their horns."

"So, you mean this could be one of your magical powers?" Lauren asked.

Twilight nodded again. "Maybe I can see what's going on in other places if I touch a rock with my horn and say what I wish to see."

"Any rock?" Lauren said excitedly.

"I don't know," Twilight replied. "But I guess there's only one way to find out." He trotted to the edge of the clearing where there was a boulder of plain gray granite. "What shall we try to see?"

"My house," Lauren suggested.

"I wish I could see Lauren's house," Twilight said, touching his horn to the stone.

Nothing happened.

"Maybe it's just when you touch a rock made out of rose quartz," Lauren said.

Twilight cantered to one of the other pinky-gray rocks and touched his horn to it. "I wish I could see Lauren's house," he said.

There was a purple flash and mist started swirling over the rock.

"It worked!" Lauren gasped. She ran over. As the mist cleared, she saw that the rock's surface was shining. An image of the outside of her house was slowly forming, blurry at first but getting sharper by the second. "Wow!" she whispered. She could see her dad's car, the path to Twilight's paddock, and Buddy,

Max's Bernese mountain dog puppy, sniffing around outside Twilight's stable.

Twilight touched his horn to the rock again and, with a slight popping noise, the picture disappeared.

Lauren went back to the first rock. The picture of Jessica's house was as clear as if she were watching it on television. Jessica was standing up now, looking very upset.

"I don't want to go shopping again tomorrow!" she said.

Her dad sighed. "Well, we're going to. It's what Samantha wants to do."

Jessica glared at him. "Why do we always have to do what she wants, Dad?" she demanded, shooting an angry look at Samantha, who was sitting on the sofa ignoring her. "It's not fair!"

"That's enough, Jessica," Mr. Parker said firmly.

Lauren saw Jessica bite back a reply and run from the room.

Mr. Parker ran a hand through his hair. "I'd better go and talk to her," he said.

Lauren turned to Twilight. "Oh, I wish we could help her. Can't you do anything?"

"What can I do?" Twilight answered.

"I don't know," Lauren admitted. She thought hard. "Maybe Mrs. Fontana will help us think of something."

Mrs. Fontana owned a bookshop and knew all about Twilight's unicorn magic.

Twilight nodded eagerly. "Good idea!"

Lauren glanced at the rock again. Sally had her arm around Samantha and was talking to her. Lauren started to lean forward to listen to what Sally was saying and then changed her mind. It somehow seemed wrong to listen in on their private conversation.

"Please, make it go away, Twilight," she said.

He touched the picture with his horn and it disappeared. Despite the light from the dancing fireflies, the clearing suddenly seemed much darker.

"Come on," Lauren said, taking hold of Twilight's mane and scrambling onto his back. "We need to get home."

CHAPTER

Six

The next morning, Lauren pushed open the old-fashioned door that led into Mrs. Fontana's bookshop. A chime jangled and Walter, Mrs. Fontana's black-and-white terrier, trotted over to greet her, his tail wagging. As Lauren patted him, Mrs. Fontana appeared from the back of the shop.

"Hello, Lauren. This is a nice

surprise," she said, coming over, a smile crinkling up her face. As always, her long gray hair was pinned up in a bun and she had a mustard-yellow shawl around her shoulders. "So, what can I do for you?"

Lauren glanced around, wondering whether it was safe to talk.

"It's OK," Mrs. Fontana said. "You're the only person in the shop." Her bright blue eyes searched Lauren's face. "I take it this visit is about Twilight?"

Lauren nodded.

"Why don't we sit down?" Mrs. Fontana said, nodding at one of the armchairs that was nestled among the piles of books — new and secondhand — that rose from the floor like wobbly towers. "So, tell me," Mrs. Fontana said, sitting opposite her. "What's the problem?"

Lauren explained about Jessica and then about the night before in the clearing. As she explained how Twilight's horn made the picture appear in the rose quartz rock, Mrs. Fontana chuckled.

"That must have given you a shock," she said.

"Yes, it did," Lauren said, grinning.

"That was always one of my favorite unicorn powers." A smile played across her face, and Lauren had the sudden feeling that Mrs. Fontana was reliving old memories. With a blink, Mrs. Fontana seemed to come back to the present. "So, what is it you want to know?"

"Can Twilight help my friend?" Lauren asked.

"Of course he can!" Mrs. Fontana smiled. "But I can't tell you how. You and Twilight must learn how to use his powers yourselves. With your good heart and his courage, I know you'll find a way."

Lauren felt disappointed. "But I've been thinking and thinking about what we can do," she said, "and I still don't know. Is there anything you can suggest?"

Mrs. Fontana's voice dropped and she leaned forward. "It might help you to know that there is a way that someone else can see Twilight. If a person drinks the Unseeing Potion, it will make them forget they have ever seen a unicorn. However" — her eyes seemed to bore into Lauren — "the Unseeing Potion will only work if it is taken knowingly and willingly. You can only reveal Twilight's secret to someone you can trust to drink the potion. If you reveal his secret to the wrong person, then his life could be in danger."

Lauren's thoughts were spinning — a potion that meant someone else could see that Twilight is a unicorn. That was amazing! A thought struck her. "But I don't see how that would help Jessica," she said.

Mrs. Fontana smiled. "As I said, how you use Twilight's powers is up to you." She seemed to see the frustration on Lauren's face. "Oh, my dear, please believe me, I am not trying to make your life difficult." She took Lauren's hands. "There is a reason why I can't tell you what Twilight's powers are or how he should use them."

"What is the reason?" Lauren asked.

Mrs. Fontana's blue gaze met hers. "One day, you will find out."

Just then, Walter gave a sharp bark. Mrs. Fontana glanced at the door. "There's someone coming," she said quickly. "We can't talk anymore now. Use the advice I have given you wisely, my dear. Promise me you will take great care before you reveal Twilight's secret to anyone."

"I will," Lauren promised.

The door opened, and Mrs. Foster looked in, holding armfuls of shopping bags. "Hello, Mrs. Fontana," she said, smiling. "There you are, Lauren," she said, catching sight of her daughter sitting in the chair. "I've bought the things I needed from town. Are you ready to go?"

Lauren nodded and got to her feet. "Bye, Mrs. Fontana."

"Good-bye, Lauren," Mrs. Fontana replied. Her eyes twinkled. "No doubt I'll see you again soon."

As Lauren reached the door, Mrs. Fontana came after her. "Oh, Lauren. You might need this." She pressed a folded piece of paper into Lauren's hand.

"Thanks," Lauren said, wondering what the note was.

Lauren quietly read the first few words to herself as they walked to the car. *Take two moonflowers and a hair from a unicorn's mane . . .*

It was the Unseeing Potion!

"What's that, honey?" her mom asked.

Lauren quickly folded up the paper and put it in her pocket. "Oh, nothing," she said quickly. "Nothing important."

CHAPTER

Seven

"I'm going to take Twilight out for a ride," Lauren said to her mom when they got home.

It only took her ten minutes to give Twilight a quick brush over and to tack him up. "Just wait till you hear what I've got to tell you," she said, as she pulled down the stirrups and mounted. "Come on — we're going to the clearing."

Sensing her excitement, Twilight pulled at the bit. As soon as they had trotted out of the farm and onto the track that led into the woods, Lauren leaned forward and let Twilight canter. His hooves thudded along the sandy track until they reached the hidden path that led to the clearing.

At the end of the path, the trees parted, and Twilight trotted into the open space. Shafts of sunlight shone down through the leafy canopy and lit up the grass. Pink-and-yellow butterflies fluttered through the air. Lauren stopped Twilight and slid off. "I'm going to turn you into a unicorn," she told him, as she started to untack him. "I know it's daytime, but no one can see us here and we need to talk."

Twilight nodded his head and snorted as if he agreed.

"OK," said Lauren, sliding the saddle off his back and putting it on the grass. "Here goes."

A few moments later, Twilight was a unicorn. It felt strange for Lauren. Until now, she'd only ever said the spell in the evening. It didn't seem right to have the sun shining down on his snowy-white coat and silvery horn. But Twilight didn't seem to find anything odd about it at all.

"So what did Mrs. Fontana say?" he asked.

"She gave me this," Lauren replied,

getting the piece of paper out of her pocket. She read out loud what Mrs. Fontana had written:

Take two moonflowers and a hair from a unicorn's mane and put them in water under the light of the moon. After ten seconds, the flowers and the hair will dissolve in the water and the potion will be ready to drink. Within thirty seconds, the person who has drunk it will have forgotten they ever saw a unicorn.

"So if someone drinks the potion they won't remember having seen me?" Twilight said.

"That's right," Lauren told him.

"But what would happen if the person changed their mind and decided not to drink the potion?" Twilight said.

"Mrs. Fontana said that was a risk," Lauren replied. "She told me that we have to be very careful about who we choose to reveal your secret to."

"But I don't understand how it would help Jessica to be able to see me," said Twilight.

Lauren sighed. "Neither do I. But I'm sure Mrs. Fontana wouldn't have given us the recipe unless it could help. I guess

we've just got to think about it a little longer." She glanced around. Although the clearing was the most secret place she could think of, there was still a chance that someone might come along. "We'd better turn you back into a pony now. I'll come and visit you tonight, and we'll see if we can think of a plan then."

"OK," Twilight agreed.

Lauren kissed his nose and then said the words of the Undoing Spell. There was a purple flash, and Twilight was a pony once more.

As Lauren rode back along the main forest path, she glanced at her watch. She might as well ride Twilight for a little bit longer.

"Let's go to Jessica's," she said to Twilight. "We won't stop for long, but it might cheer her up to see us."

Twilight nodded, and they trotted along the road to Jessica's house.

Sally was watering the pots of flowers at the front of the house. "Hello, Lauren," she said, smiling as Lauren turned Twilight into the driveway. "Have you come to see Jessica?"

"Yes," Lauren said, thinking how nice Sally was. "I just thought I'd say hi."

"I'll go and get her," Sally said. "And maybe your pony would like some water? I could get a bucket from the backyard."

"That would be great," Lauren said, smiling at her and dismounting.

Sally went into the house. A minute later, Jessica came running out of the front door. "Lauren! Sally said you were here. Oh, Twilight," she said, giving him a hug. He nuzzled her, leaving a messy mark on her T-shirt. Jessica grinned, not seeming to mind a bit.

"It's really good to see you," she said to Lauren.

"How's it going?" Lauren asked her anxiously. Although Jessica was smiling now, her eyes looked suspiciously red, as if she'd recently been crying.

"Oh, it's not too bad," Jessica said. She spoke bravely, but Lauren could tell she was upset. "I've got to go and try on a bridesmaid's dress this afternoon," Jessica continued. She swallowed, then burst out, "Oh, Lauren, I just don't want the wedding to happen! Samantha was so mean last night."

Lauren only just stopped herself from saying "I know."

"Um . . . how?" Lauren asked.

"Oh, the usual," Jessica said. "I got a little mad, and Dad lectured me. He said I've got to try to be more understanding. He said that he knows Samantha seems difficult to get along with, but it's just because she's upset about leaving her school and friends to come and live here. But I think it's because she just doesn't like me!"

"Of course she does," Lauren started to say. "Maybe your dad has a point —"

"But she *doesn't* like me, Lauren!" Jessica

interrupted, her blue eyes welling with tears. "And I don't want to live with her!"

Just then, the back gate opened and Sally came out with a bucket of water and a couple of carrots. "Here we are," she said cheerfully. "I thought he might be hungry as well."

"Thanks," Lauren said, glancing at Jessica, who had hidden her face from Sally by stroking Twilight's neck.

"Well," Sally said, putting down the bucket. "I'll leave you two alone, then. Don't stay out here too long, Jessica. Remember we've got your bridesmaid's dress fitting this afternoon."

Jessica nodded.

As Sally went inside, Lauren looked anxiously at Jessica. "Are you OK?"

Jessica sniffed. "I guess I'll have to be,"

she said in a small voice. "See you, Lauren. I wish this wedding wasn't happening."

Lauren sighed. If only she could think of some way of helping . . .

The minutes seemed to crawl by very slowly until the evening. Lauren wished she could go and talk things over with Twilight. As soon as she and Max had finished filling the dishwasher with their dirty plates, Lauren put on her sneakers. "I'm just going to see Twilight," she said to her parents.

"OK, honey," her dad said. He looked under the kitchen table, where Max was playing with Buddy. "Come on, Max. Time for your bath."

Just as he and Max were going up the stairs, the phone rang. "Lauren, can you get that for me, please?" he called.

Lauren jumped to her feet and picked up the receiver. "Granger's Farm. Who's speaking, please?"

"Lauren. It's Jessica's dad here." Mr. Parker's voice was tense and tight, and in the background Lauren was sure she could hear someone crying.

"Oh, hello," Lauren started to say, wondering why he was calling. "Do you want to speak to my —"

Mr. Parker cut her off. "Lauren, have

you seen Jessica in the last couple of hours?"

Lauren frowned. "No. Why?"

"She's missing," Mr. Parker said. "We think she ran away!"

CHAPTER

Eight

For a moment, Lauren was too shocked to speak. "Ran away?" she stammered at last.

"Can I speak to your father, please?" Mr. Parker asked.

"Dad!" Lauren shouted.

Mr. Foster came hurrying down the stairs. "What's the matter?" he asked, seeing her pale face.

"Jessica ran away!" Lauren exclaimed.

Her dad took the phone. Lauren's legs felt shaky, and she sat down at the table. It was still light outside at the moment, but soon it would get dark. What would Jessica do then?

"I'll come over and help you look, Jack," she heard her father saying quickly. "I'll tell Alice what's happening. She can call if Jessica turns up here." There was a pause, and then Mr. Foster nodded. "Sure. I'll get there as soon as I can."

He put the phone down.

"Can I come with you?" Lauren asked, jumping to her feet.

"I think it's best if you stay here," Mr. Foster said. "Everyone at the Parkers' is very upset just now — particularly Samantha. Mr. Parker said she seems to think it's all her fault."

Mr. Foster saw the worry on his daughter's face and gave her a quick hug. "It'll be all right," he said comfortingly. "We'll find Jessica. Don't worry."

Five minutes later, Lauren was alone in the kitchen. Her mom and Max were upstairs and her dad had gone to the Parkers'. She went to the window and stared out into the dusk. If only she knew where Jessica was.

And it was then that an idea struck her. Of course! Twilight's magic powers could show her. They only had to look into the rock. Why hadn't she thought of it before?

She pulled open the door and raced outside.

"Twilight!" she cried, running down the path to the paddock. "Quick! I need your help."

Twilight was already standing by the gate. He began to whinny frantically.

"Jessica's missing," she gasped. "We need to go to the clearing and —"

A neigh from Twilight cut across her words. He reared up, his front hooves stamping down on the grass.

"What's the matter?" Lauren asked in astonishment. The only other time she'd ever seen him looking so agitated was when Max and Buddy had almost caught her turning him into a unicorn. Her eyes suddenly widened. Maybe there was someone nearby?

She spun around, half-expecting to see someone, but there were only the familiar shapes of the trees and bushes, shadowy against the night sky.

"What is it?" she asked Twilight.

Twilight stamped his front hoof. Lauren listened. In the silence, she heard a sudden rustle.

Her heart almost jumped out of her chest. The noise had come from a large bush near the gate. Taking a deep breath, she walked forward. "Hello?" she called, trying to sound brave. "Is there anyone there?"

Through the silence of the night came the sound of a sob. Lauren ran forward, suddenly no longer afraid. She reached into the bush and pushed the branches aside.

"Jessica!" she gasped.

Jessica was crouching in the hollow center of the bush. Her face was streaked with tears. When she saw Lauren she buried her head in her hands and sobbed again.

"What are you doing here?" Lauren asked.

Jessica showed no signs of answering and so Lauren pushed her way through the brambles toward her. "Please come out." She put an arm around Jessica's shoulders and helped her out of the bush. Twilight came over and nuzzled Jessica's cold hands.

"Everyone's looking for you," Lauren said, staring at her friend. "What's wrong?"

"Everything." Jessica put her arms around Twilight's neck and buried her face in his mane. "I don't want to go home ever again, Lauren."

"Why? What's happened?" Lauren asked.

Jessica sniffed. "This afternoon was awful. We went to try the bridesmaids' dresses on, and Samantha refused to wear the shoes or hats that we had chosen, and

then she said that I'm just a little kid who doesn't know anything. Then she wouldn't speak to her mom because Sally said that my opinion *did* matter. Worst of all, when we got home, Dad said he and Sally have decided that when Samantha moves in after the wedding, she's going to share my bedroom."

"Share your bedroom?" Lauren echoed.

Jessica nodded. "Dad says that they think it will help us get to know each other better. But I don't want to get to know Samantha," she wailed. "She hates me, and I bet she's glad I ran away."

Lauren shook her head. "She's not — she's really upset."

"As if," Jessica said.

"She is," Lauren insisted. "Your dad said."

"It's just an act, then," Jessica said. "She doesn't care about me at all." And with that, she began to cry again.

Lauren hugged her, wishing that she could show Jessica that Samantha did care.

Twilight whinnied. Lauren looked at him. He turned to look in the direction of the woods.

Lauren caught her breath. Of course! There actually was a way that she could show Jessica that Samantha was upset. But it would mean revealing Twilight's secret.

Leaving Jessica for a moment, Lauren went over to Twilight. "Are you sure?" she whispered into his ear.

Twilight nickered softly and nodded his head.

"OK," Lauren told him. She turned to her friend. "Jessica, I'm sure I can prove that Samantha really does care about you."

Jessica frowned. "How?"

"I'll tell you in a second," Lauren said. "But first you have to promise that afterward you'll do whatever I ask."

Jessica gave Lauren a long look. "All right," Jessica said. "I promise."

Lauren swallowed. "OK." She took Jessica's hand. "Look, don't be scared, but Twilight isn't just a pony, Jessica. He's . . . well . . ." She took a breath. "He's a unicorn."

For a moment, Jessica looked at her in

stunned silence and then, despite her unhappiness, she laughed. "A unicorn!" she said. "Don't be silly, Lauren!"

"No, he really is," Lauren said.

Jessica stared at her. "Unicorns don't exist. They're just make-believe —"

"Just watch," Lauren interrupted. She turned around and quickly said the magic spell. Suddenly, Twilight was standing there — a unicorn once more.

Lauren thought Jessica was going to faint.

"But . . . but . . ." Jessica stammered, staring at him, her eyes wide.

"See, unicorns *do* exist," Lauren said.

Jessica walked slowly to Twilight. "He's so beautiful!" With a shaking hand, she reached out and touched his neck. "Oh, wow!" she breathed. "Just wait till everyone hears about this!"

"You can't tell anyone, Jessica," Lauren said quickly. "It has to be a secret."

Jessica frowned. "But I don't understand," she said.

"We'll talk about it later," Lauren said. Time was passing and, with every minute that went by, she knew that Jessica's family would be getting more and more worried. First, she had to complete her plan, then she and Twilight had to get Jessica home as quickly as they could. She looked at Twilight. "Can you carry us both?"

"Yes, of course," Twilight said.

Jessica almost jumped out of her skin.

"You can only hear him if you're touching him or holding a hair from his mane," Lauren told her. She saw Jessica's mouth start to open with a question. "Come on, I'll explain on the way."

As Twilight flew to the clearing in the woods, Lauren told Jessica all about unicorns and how she had discovered Twilight's secret. Jessica was thrilled. "So there are other unicorns in the world?" she said as Twilight began to fly down through the trees.

"Yes," Lauren said. "But they just look like gray ponies. They can only turn into a unicorn if they find someone who believes in magic enough to say the Turning Spell."

"Like you did," Jessica said, as Twilight landed on the soft grass.

Lauren nodded and dismounted.

"I'd give anything to have a unicorn of my own," Jessica said longingly. She slid off Twilight's back and looked around at the fireflies dancing through the dimly lit clearing. "What a cool place," she breathed. "But why are we here?"

"We're going to show you how Samantha really feels about you," Lauren said, walking over to one of the pinky-gray rocks. She desperately hoped that her plan was going to work.

Twilight joined her. "I wish I could

see Samantha," she said, and Twilight touched the stone with his horn.

Jessica gasped as the purple light flashed, and the mist started to swirl. She grabbed Lauren's arm.

"It's OK," Lauren told her. "Watch what happens now."

Just as before, the mist slowly cleared to show the surface of the rock beginning to shine like a mirror. As they watched, two shadowy shapes in the mirror gradually became clearer.

"It's Samantha and Sally!" Jessica exclaimed in astonishment.

The mirror showed a picture of the kitchen at Jessica's house. Samantha and her mom were sitting at the table.

"You need to get close to be able to hear
what they're saying," Lauren said to Jessica.
They crouched down together.

"She's been gone for hours now,

Mom," Samantha was sobbing. "What if she doesn't come back?"

"She will," Sally soothed, stroking her hair. "I'm sure Jack will find her soon."

"But what if he doesn't? Oh, Mom, it's all my fault," Samantha cried. "I was so mean to her. I wish I hadn't been. It's just that I've been so scared about coming to live here. It's Jessica's life and Jessica's house, and I feel like an outsider."

"I know, Sam," her mom said. "But our house is too far away from Jack's work for us to live there." She stroked her hair. "I promise it won't take you long to settle in and make new friends here. And I'm sure Jessica will help you."

"If she ever comes back," Samantha

said. "What if something bad happened to her?" More tears spilled out of her eyes. "Oh, Mom, I'm so worried."

Sally hugged Samantha tight, but as she lifted her eyes upward, Lauren could see how strained and worried she looked.

Lauren glanced at Jessica. Her face was pale and she looked shocked. Lauren reached out and took her hand. "See? It won't be that bad when your dad and Sally get married," she said softly. "And maybe having a sister will be fun."

Jessica swallowed hard and looked at Twilight. "Can you show me what it will be like?" she asked.

Twilight shook his head. "No one can see into the future, not even unicorns."

He nuzzled her shoulder. "The future's up to you, Jessica. It's what you make of it. But now that you know how Samantha feels, I'm sure it will all work out — if you want it to."

Jessica took a deep breath. "I want it to," she said. She glanced at the mirror again. "There's Dad," she said suddenly. "Look!"

Mr. Parker had just come into the picture. Lauren and Jessica both bent forward to hear what was going on.

Sally had jumped to her feet. "Have you found her?"

Mr. Parker shook his head. "I thought I'd check back here to see if she called."

Sally shook her head. "No . . . no, she hasn't."

Mr. Parker ran his hand through his hair. "Where is she?" he groaned. "It's the wedding. I know it is."

"Maybe we should call it off," Sally said, looking worried.

"No!" Jessica exclaimed. She looked at Lauren and Twilight. Her eyes were suddenly glinting with tears. "Take me home, Twilight," she said. "Please!"

CHAPTER

Nine

As Jessica clambered onto Twilight's snowy-white back, Lauren bent down and picked two purple moonflowers from the grass. She felt a flutter of fear. Was Jessica going to keep her promise to do whatever Lauren asked when they took her home?

The flight home was tense. Lauren could sense how anxious Jessica was to let her family know that she was safe. It seemed like forever before Twilight landed gently under the cover of some trees near Jessica's house.

"We need to stop a minute," Lauren told Jessica as they dismounted.

"But I want to get home as quickly as possible," Jessica said.

"It'll only take a minute," Lauren assured her. "We need to do something first."

"What?" Jessica asked.

Lauren took a deep breath. "Well, you remember that before I turned Twilight into a unicorn I made you promise that you would do whatever I asked?" she said.

"Yes," Jessica said.

"Well, you've got to drink a potion

that will make you forget you've ever seen that Twilight is a unicorn. That's what this water is for," she said, taking a little bottle out of her pocket. "It's to make the potion."

"I won't remember anything about him at all?" Jessica said a little sadly.

Lauren shook her head.

"But . . . but . . ." Jessica seemed lost for words.

"It's to keep him safe," Lauren said. "If anyone else knows about him, he could be in real danger."

"I think I understand," Jessica said slowly.

"So you'll drink the potion?" Lauren asked her.

Jessica nodded. "Yes," she said.

"Well, all I need to do is add the flowers and a hair from Twilight's mane to this water," Lauren said. "And then we put it in the moonlight for ten seconds and it's ready to drink."

She broke off a single hair from Twilight's mane and dropped it into the bottle with the two flowers. The water immediately fizzed and bubbled and turned purple. Lauren held it up to a shaft of moonlight that was filtering down through the trees. As they watched, the purple faded and the liquid became clear. A sweet smell floated off it, like lemonade.

"It's ready," Lauren said, after she had

counted to ten. She held the bottle out to
Jessica.

Jessica stroked the unicorn's neck.

"Good-bye, Twilight," she said softly. Twilight blew gently on her face, and then she took the bottle. "Here goes," she said, and in one gulp she drained the liquid.

Lauren watched her. She sort of expected something to happen — a purple flash or something — but nothing did.

"Thank you," Jessica said, handing the bottle back to Lauren. "It tasted sort of sweet and fruity." She frowned. "But it didn't make me forget about Twilight."

"The spell said that it takes thirty seconds to work," Twilight said.

Lauren looked toward the house. "You'd better go," she said to Jessica. The kitchen curtains weren't closed, and she could see Mr. Parker pacing up and down while Sally hugged Samantha at the kitchen table. "Everyone's worried about you. Let them know you're all right."

"OK," Jessica said. "Bye!" And with that she began to run across the lawn. But just as she reached the back door, she stopped.

"What's she doing?" Lauren whispered to Twilight as Jessica looked around in a confused way.

"I think the potion just worked," he said softly.

As they watched, Jessica shook her head and ran into the house.

From the shelter of the trees, Twilight and Lauren watched the kitchen window.

They saw the worry on Mr. Parker's face disappear in an instant as Jessica ran into the room. Sally and Samantha jumped to their feet in relief. And they saw Jessica being pulled into a big family hug.

Lauren swallowed the lump of happy tears in her throat. "Oh, Twilight, I think life's going to be better for Jessica from now on," she said.

He stamped his hoof. "I think you're right," he replied.

Two weeks later, Lauren rode Twilight up to Jessica's house. A big white car was parked in their driveway and, as Lauren halted Twilight to have a look at it, the front door of the house opened and

Jessica and Samantha ran out. They were dressed in cream-colored bridesmaid's dresses and they were smiling.

"They're never going to get there on time," Lauren heard Samantha say.

"Dad's always late!" Jessica said to Samantha.

"That makes two of them," Samantha told her.

Jessica laughed. Lauren didn't think she'd ever seen her friend look happier. "Dad! We're going to be late!" Jessica shouted.

The door opened wider and Sally and Mr. Parker appeared. Sally was dressed in a beautiful light-blue dress and Mr. Parker was wearing a brand-new gray suit.

"Come on!" Jessica insisted, taking

hold of her dad's arm and dragging him
to the car.

Just then, Sally caught sight of Lauren.
"Hi!" she called, waving. "Jessica — it's
Lauren!"

Jessica came racing over. "Lauren! Lauren!" she gasped. "Dad's just told me the best news. He's going to get Samantha and me a pony as a wedding present. It turns out she loves horses just as much as I do!"

"That's wonderful!" Lauren exclaimed.

Mr. Parker beeped the car's horn. "Jessica! You'll make us late!"

Jessica looked indignant. "Me? Make you late?"

Samantha leaned out of the window. "Hi, Lauren. Come on, Jessica!"

"I'd better go," Jessica said to Lauren. She reached to pat Twilight good-bye and suddenly a puzzled look crossed her face. She frowned, almost as if she was trying to remember something. "You know, I had this really funny dream about Twilight . . ." she began.

The car's horn sounded. Jessica's expression cleared. "Oh, it doesn't matter," she said, shaking her head. "See you at school!" And with that, she ran to the car.

As Jessica got in, Lauren waved and Twilight whinnied. Then the car pulled out of the driveway and set off down the road.

Lauren looked at Twilight and smiled. The potion really had worked. Once again, only she knew that her pony was a unicorn in disguise. Their secret was safe for now.

My Secret Unicorn

Starlight Surprise

Touching her heels to Twilight's sides, Lauren rode him down the overgrown path. As they got nearer, the tree house seemed to loom up in front of them. Its old gray walls were covered with green moss and the air around it seemed still and silent. A shiver ran down Lauren's spine. It did look kind of spooky. Her heart started to beat faster. It couldn't really be haunted, could it?

Twilight has a mystery to solve after dark

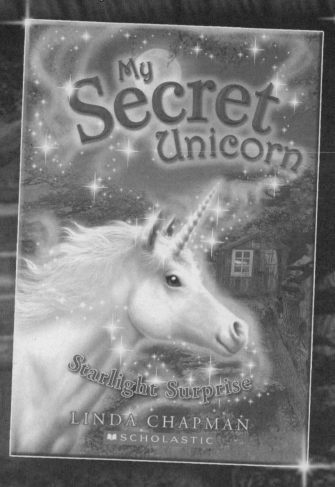

My **Secret** Unicorn

Starlight Surprise

LINDA CHAPMAN

■SCHOLASTIC

Lauren doesn't believe in ghosts, but there is
definitely something spooky going on down by the creek.
Then one night, as Lauren and Twilight fly over the woods
near the scary tree house, they make a surprising discovery.

■ SCHOLASTIC

www.scholastic.com

MSU